# Worlds I Know
## and Other Poems

*Also by Myra Cohn Livingston*

CELEBRATIONS

THE CHILD AS POET:
MYTH OR REALITY?

A CIRCLE OF SEASONS

COME AWAY
(*A Margaret K. McElderry Book*)

A LOLLYGAG OF LIMERICKS
(*A Margaret K. McElderry Book*)

THE MALIBU AND OTHER POEMS
(*A Margaret K. McElderry Book*)

NO WAY OF KNOWING: DALLAS POEMS
(*A Margaret K. McElderry Book*)

O SLIVER OF LIVER AND OTHER POEMS
(*A Margaret K. McElderry Book*)

SKY SONGS

A SONG I SANG TO YOU

THE WAY THINGS ARE AND OTHER POEMS
(*A Margaret K. McElderry Book*)

MONKEY PUZZLE AND OTHER POEMS
(*A Margaret K. McElderry Book*)


*Edited by Myra Cohn Livingston*

CALLOOH! CALLAY!
HOLIDAY POEMS FOR YOUNG READERS
(*A Margaret K. McElderry Book*)

HOW PLEASANT TO KNOW MR. LEAR!

O FRABJOUS DAY!
POETRY FOR HOLIDAYS AND SPECIAL OCCASIONS
(*A Margaret K. McElderry Book*)

POEMS OF CHRISTMAS
(*A Margaret K. McElderry Book*)

POEMS OF LEWIS CARROLL

WHY AM I GROWN SO COLD?
POEMS OF THE UNKNOWABLE
(*A Margaret K. McElderry Book*)

A LEARICAL LEXICON
(*A Margaret K. McElderry Book*)

# WORLDS I KNOW
## And Other Poems

*Myra Cohn Livingston*

*Drawings by Tim Arnold*

*A Margaret K. McElderry Book*
Atheneum 1985 New York

*To Mother, again,*
*for*
*January 14, 1984*

*Library of Congress Cataloging in Publication Data*

Livingston, Myra Cohn.
Worlds I know and other poems.
"A Margaret K. McElderry book."
Summary: A collection of poems reflecting special
feelings and events of childhood, including a toboggan
ride, a Christmas play, and the love of special objects.
1. Children's poetry, American. [1. American poetry]
I. Arnold, Tim, ill. II. Title.
PS3562.I945W6 1985     811'.54     85-7344
ISBN 0-689-50332-6

Published simultaneously in Canada by Collier Macmillan Canada, Inc.
Composition by Heritage Printers, Inc.,
Charlotte, North Carolina
Manufactured by Fairfield Graphics,
Fairfield, Pennsylvania
First Edition

# Contents

## Toboggan Ride: Down Happy Hollow

Cold that day
we started down
tobogganing
the snowy ground;
held our breath
around a tree
and Shirley Ann
squeezed tight to me;
Laura yelled,
as we flew past
one crazy kid,
his skis half-smashed,
and Margie steered
around a sled
until
until
I felt my head
go spinning round
in sprays of snow

and Margie said
she just let go
the steering—
it was all a joke—
until she found
her glasses, broke,
and Shirley Ann
began to cry,
and Laura laughed—

so that's when I
made sure that all

was clear below
and laid myself
down in the snow
and made myself
all stiff and tight
and started rolling
out of sight
and never laughed
or cried
until
I reached
the bottom
of the
hill.

## Bert

I have to be nice.
His dad knows my dad.
But he's short and he's ugly
and always acts bad.

Even Miss Teich
has to scold him in class.
Once, when he found
an old piece of green glass,

he carved his initials
and mine—on a tree.
He does things like that
to embarrass me.

Once, he got scissors
and cut off his hair,
and if I look over my desk
he'll just stare

and do funny things
with his nose and his ears,
and say awful words
when Miss Teich isn't near.

I don't understand
why he has to be bad
and I wish that his dad
wasn't friends with my dad.

## Christmas Play

We had shepherds
and a paper star
and straw spread all around.
Maria fixed a box to make a manger
on the ground.
Kim and Tracy brought their dolls,
Melinda brought another,
but none of them looked holy,
so Meg loaned her little brother.
Mike was keeper of the inn.
Joseph, that was Barry.
And since she brought the newborn babe
Meg was the Virgin Mary.

*Doll*

The Christmas
when my sister came

she got a doll
without a name

and so I helped her out
and chose

*Samantha*

and put on her clothes
and dressed her up
and curled her hair.
I took Samantha everywhere

and hid her underneath the bed
so she could be my doll instead.

## The Marionettes

Patton and Dick
make marionettes.
Friday, they let me see
the way they string up the wood controls
and the place where the knots have to be.

Patton knows
how to saw the wood,
and Dick is the one who sews.
They both make the heads out of papier-maché,
and they both write the words for their shows.

One time
they let me go backstage
while they were rehearsing their lines.
They let me start the music once,
but not any other times.

Two is enough,
they say, to work,
or everything gets in a mess.
But once I brought them a piece of silk
for the princess's ballroom dress,

And they let me make
a foil crown
and watch—while Dick glued it in place.
And they said I could stay for half an hour
when I found them a bit of lace.

Patton and Dick

make marionettes
for the Great Klopp & Campbell Show.
And every Saturday afternoon
I sit in the very first row.

## Kittens

Our cat had kittens
weeks ago
when everything outside was snow.

So she stayed in
and kept them warm
and safe from all the clouds and storm.

But yesterday
when there was sun
she snuzzled on the smallest one

and turned it over
from beneath
and took its fur between her teeth

and carried it
outside to see
how nice a winter day can be

and then our dog
decided he
would help her take the other three

and one by one
they took them out
to see what sun is all about

so when they're grown
they'll always know
to never be afraid of snow.

## May Day

On May Day
I was Maypole Queen.
I wore
a long
white
gown.
It turned
all brown
and muddy
from the rain
left
on the ground.

My golden wand
got broken
when we danced
the ribbons
round,
but the clover
and the daisies
are still
twining
in my
crown.

*Aunts and Uncles*

Aga,
 Zelda,
  Ruth and
  Flora,
   Becky,
    Blanche,
     Anna,
      Cora,
       Rosie,
       Rae,
        Irma,
         Grace

      every aunt has a different face.

Irving,
 John,
  Harry,
   Milton,
    Walter,
     Ed,
      Abe and
      Nathan,
       Victor,
        Carl,
         Joe and
         Lee

      every uncle belongs to me.

## The Gypsies

There
by the spring
in Elmwood Park
where the trees grow tall
and the shade grows dark,
the gypsies
come to fill their cans,
in painted trucks
and curtained vans,
and they carry water
up the stair,
their singing
ringing
through the air.

All
summer long
the gypsies bring
their cans and pails
down
to the spring,
the men with scarves
around their heads;
the ladies' lips
are painted red,
their skirts swirl out
and touch the ground
with sequins
glittering
around.

And
once I saw a lady
rest
for a bit
where the watercress
grows green and sweet
on a summer day.
She picked a bunch
and started away
when a gold-tooth man
with a ring in his ear
came to look
in the waters clear,
to see himself
in the mirror spring.
The lady stopped,
and I saw her fling
him the bunch
of the cress she took,
and he started up
and gave her a look.
And they laughed
to each other
there
in the park
and walked away
where the shade
grows
dark.

## Mother's Garden

Mother's
in the garden
all the time that she can go.
She likes to plant her pansies
in a curvy sort of row.
She has to clip the bridal wreath
and prune the little trees.
She has a special trowel to use
and gets down on her knees
for pinks
and bachelor buttons
that she's planted
in the rocks.
And one year
when the flowers came
there were six hollyhocks
and the blossoms sort of puckered up
and fell down in the dirt,
and she showed me how
they twirl around
like dancing ladies' skirts;
and how to pinch snapdragons
so they almost seem to talk,
and how the dandelions blow
their puffs
along the walk,
and the beard that's on the iris,
and how baby seeds come up,
and the golden dust
that powders
in the first spring
buttercup.

## Saturday

On Saturdays
we sometimes go
to lunch at the El Patio.

Dad says
I've worked hard long enough
with all his envelopes to stuff,

so then we walk
up Farnam Street
and find the place we like to eat,

and there's a table
where we sit
and order two big French rolls split

and filled
with peanut butter, sliced
banana and some lemon ice,

and drink our milk,
and when we're through
we still have lots of work to do,

so we walk back
down to Dad's store,
and after that I stuff some more

until my Mother
comes for me,
and then my Saturday is free.

*Worlds I Know*

I can read the pictures
by myself
in the books that lie
on the lowest shelf.
I know the place
where the stories start
and some I can even say
by heart,
and I make up adventures
and dreams and words
for some of the pages
I've never heard.

But I like it best
when Mother sits
and reads to me
my favorites;
when Rapunzel pines
and the prince comes forth,
or the Snow Queen sighs
in the bitter north;
when Rose Red snuggles
against the bear,
and I lean against Mother
and feel her hair.

We look at stars
in Hungary—
back of the North Wind—
over the sea—
the Nutcracker laughs;

the Erl King calls;
a wish comes true;
the beanstalk falls;
the Western wind
blows sweet and low,
and Mother gives words
to worlds I know.

## Secret Door

The upstairs room
has a secret door.
Dad says someone
used it for
some papers many years ago,
and if I want to, I can go
and bring a treasured thing
to hide
and lock it up
all dark inside

and it can be
a place for me
to open
with
its
tiny
key.

*Sleep–Over*

Marian
said
to pretend to sleep
and wait for her mother to go,
and then we could talk
the whole night long
and no one would ever know.

Marian
said
that the spooks come out
and climb through the window at night,
and she screamed four times
and woke everyone up
and she left on the bathroom light.

Marian
said
that the closet has ghosts
and she put a chalk hex on the door.
I slept over three times
at Marian's house,
but I'm not going there anymore.

## Mosquitoes

Out on the porch,
near the light,
mosquitoes dance
and hum
and bite

and itch my arms
into red rings,
and the stuff
Mom puts on them
smarts and stings.

Both of my legs
have ugly spots
and welts of
pinkish
polka dots,

so all through summer,
every week,
I smell like
a bottle
of campho-phenique,

and what isn't red
is a chalky pink
from the calamine lotion
that makes me
stink,

but it's better
than staying in
at night

when mosquitoes dance
around the light.

## Grandfather Clock

The
grandfather
clock
stands
dark
and
tall
against
the
stucco
of
the
wall

with
the
face
of a
smiling
sun
by day
and a
staring
moon
when
the sun
goes away

and a pendulum
in a window of flowers
and a voice of music
telling the hours.

## My Cousins' Dollhouse

In the dollhouse
in the brown room
sits a doll
with braided hair.
Soon she'll leave
her velvet sofa
and go walking
to her chair
in the bedroom
near the nursery
where her children
are in bed;
then she'll fix her husband dinner
and they'll eat their meat and bread.

In the dollhouse
Uncle Harry
built
in secret
through the nights,
there are windows
filled with curtains;
there are real
electric lights;
there are goblets
blown in Venice;
there are doilies made of lace.
Every day the dinner table
has the silverware in place.

And when
Harriet is older,

and when
Frances says I may,
Santa Claus
will come
and move it
to my room
where it can stay.
It will have
the velvet sofa;
it will have
the bedroom chair;
it will have
the children sleeping
and the doll with braided hair.

## Bats

Versa says
on August nights
we'd best beware
the minute lights
start switching on,
and look up high
to where the poplars
lace the sky.

Versa says
that hiding there,
just waiting,
waiting everywhere,
are hanging bats
that swoop so quick
we have to run,
or else they stick
and tangle up
inside our hair
and flap their sticky wings
in there
and twitter
bats things in our ears,
so someone has to find
long shears
and cut them out
and cut our hair.

Versa says
we'd best beware
and stay indoors

without the lights
for fear of bats
on August nights.

## The Dark

It's always
dark
around my bed,
and darkest
where I put my head;
and there are nights
when strange sounds
call
inside
the hollow
of the wall
and creaking noises
from inside
the closet
where
the
nightmares
hide;
so after I have said
my prayers
and hear them
talking from
downstairs,
I look around
so I can see
where everything
I know
should be—
especially
along the floor,
the crack of light
beneath the door.

*Harney Street*

Great-Aunt Anna
is scary—
she looks like a witch,
her teeth big and yellow
as old piano keys;
and Ruby's
a dwarf
who just laughs at herself
and runs up the stairs
every time
she sees me;
Ethel
knows Latin,
and everyone says
she's smarter
than anyone else in the world;
Ronald's so tall
he bends over himself;
and Helen's head
bounces,
she's so tightly
curled.

We have to go
visit them
once in a while
and say that we're happy
to see them—

but Dad
can
always
find reasons

to say goodbye
quickly
and leave
Ruby
laughing,

and
that
makes me
glad.

## The Grandfather I Never Knew

The grandfather
I never knew
was very thin
with eyes of blue
and traveled off
on lots of trips,
on trains and planes
and ocean ships.

And he took Nanny, too,
until
in California
he was ill,
and though she says
the doctors tried,
he was too sick
and so he died.

And I was just
a baby then,
and so I can't remember
when
they took his picture
holding me—
the grandfather
I'll never see.

## Nanny

Nanny rode on a camel
in Egypt
and sailed on a boat
up the Nile.
But the picture of her
on a camel
doesn't show she has much
of a smile.

Nanny went to a place
in Paris.
There's a picture of her
on the stair,
but the place is all busy
with people
so it's hard to make out if
she's there.

She has pictures
of London
and Venice
and a lot of old cities
like that.
In Rome there are pictures of Nanny
with a pigeon
on top of her hat.

Nanny keeps all her pictures
together
in an album
and shows them to me,
and tells me about

my grandfather,
remembering
how things used to be.

## Shell

When it was time
for Show and Tell,
Adam brought a big pink shell.

He told about
the ocean roar
and walking on the sandy shore.

And then he passed
the shell around.
We listened to the water sound.

And that's the first time
I could hear
the wild waves calling to my ear.

## Aunt Evelyn

She lives in Chicago.
I want to go there
and visit Aunt Evelyn
on East Delaware,
and sleep in the guest room
and ride on the bus
and do all the things
that she plans
just for us.

She's my aunt with blue eyes
and with gold in her hair,
and she has the most beautiful dresses
to wear,
and she lives in a place
on the very top floor
where we get to ride up
with the man
at the door.

One day we have lunch
at a fancy hotel,
and we look at the lake
and we ride on the El,
and she bought me some handkerchiefs,
one for each day,
with my name written on,
and a new game
to play.

Both my cousins are babies
who play in the park,

and my uncle comes home from his work
after dark,
so Aunt Evelyn's all mine
when I'm visiting there,
with the blue in her eyes
and the gold
in her hair.

## From Council Bluffs to Omaha

Across the river is Iowa,
You can tell by the bluffs and trees.
You can see when you drive across the bridge
to the other bank and look at the ridge
rising up from the muddy bed.
Lincoln stood there once, they said.
That is Council Bluffs.

Nebraska's on the other side.
All that keeps them apart
is the bridge you travel in a car
and the big Missouri. It isn't far
when you get downtown and turn to the right
and all the buildings come in sight.
That is Omaha.

## Indians of the Plains

I like the names,
the way they sound—

> Omaha, Iowa, Sioux,
> Pawnee, Winnebago, Potawatomi,
>
> Indian tribes who knew
> these prairies before we came,
> who lived with the buffalo—
> Illinois, Osage, Sauk
> > who lived
>
> on plains of long ago.

## Lincoln Park

If you go up North Second
and walk to the left
you can see where Lincoln stood.

There's a monument there
put up for him—
Abe Lincoln, honest and good.

Some say he came
to look at the land
that he won for a settlement.

Some say he came
for the railroad lines
before he was President.

But when he came visiting
Council Bluffs,
he stood at this place and looked down.

And I think about,
before I was born,
when Abe Lincoln came to town.

*Mary Lorenz*

Mary Lorenz
came down from the farm
and lived off the upstairs hall.
She hung a wood cross over her bed.
Every Sunday she'd cover her head
and go off to church
and tell her beads
and say a prayer for us all.

Mary Lorenz
left us one day
and went off to join the nuns.
She writes me letters to tell me how
it is to take on a holy vow,
and I should be good
and remember about
the good times we had once.

Mary Lorenz
is far away
and tells me I shouldn't cry.
She sent me a prayer card to put in my books
and a picture of her and how she looks
in her novice habit,
and writes how she'll be
a sister two years from July.

Mary Lorenz
says her convent is fine,
it's a beautiful place to be.
But I miss the wood cross over her bed
and the secrets we knew and the jokes we said

when she was with us,
so I pray she'll come back
and be in her room for me.

## Old Sam

Below the bluffs
on the river bed
the muddy Missouri
flows.

There in summer,
brown as dried grass,
Old Sam, the beggar,
goes,

Stiff brown boots
laced up to his knees,
torn away at the
toes,

he shuffles along
the cracked dry earth,
dirt stuck to his
clothes.

Where Old Sam lives
in the winter cold
no one ever
knows,

so it's only in summer
we look for him
where the brown Missouri
flows.

## Aunt Ruth

Aunt Ruth
took sick
when she was little.
Now her bones are bent.
Now her smile is strange and crooked.

Now her days
are spent
under blankets
where she lies there
quiet
in her bed,
with a picture of a lady
high
above
her head.

Once I
picked her
wildflowers,
but her hands
were weak.
So I put them
on the table;
though she
couldn't speak
I could tell
her eyes
were looking
for a long, long while,
and I saw her sad lips changing
to a
twisted smile.

On
the sunporch
is a wheelchair.
Gran says
Aunt Ruth used to go
riding
when someone could take her
down
the
hillside
very slow.
Gran says that when Aunt Ruth's better,
if she wants to—
then, maybe—
if I ask her very gently,
Aunt Ruth will go out with me.

## Party

Just before
they go downtown—
Mother in her long blue gown
and Daddy in his dressed-up tux—
he gives her a flower box
with pink carnations
and a pin,
and Mother holds them to her skin
and to her hair
and to her dress
and asks him
which he likes the best;
and then he helps her pin them on.
She ties his tie
and they are gone.

And all that's left
after the rush
is flower tissue,
soft to crush,
and curly ribbon
lying there
for me to wind
around my hair;
and near the mirror
in their room
a garden smell
of faint perfume.

## Grandfather

Grandfather
sits
in his chair
in the hall,
dark as the night
when the barn owls call;
lost in the pattern
of leaves on the wall;
sitting out there,
alone.

Grandfather
tells
how the old
songs go;
how to herd cattle
and make corn grow;
how all the Indians
hunted buffalo;
all of the things
he's
known.

Grandfather
keeps
an old sword from the war;
the blanket an Osage chief
once wore;
a moose head hung high
over his door;
and a hide-scraper
made of

bone.

Grandfather
speaks
of the lands far away:
Samoa, China,
Spain,
Bombay;
all of the places
he'll see one day;
all the skies
unknown.

Grandfather
nods,
his hands on his chest,
dreaming his dreams
of East and West;
taking
a little bit of a rest,
lost in a place
of his
own.

## Basket

Grandmother's basket
of ribbon and lace
is kept in a high-up closet place.

But when I go over
she'll take it out
and let me rummage all about

and find materials. I can choose
whatever Grandmother doesn't use

when she knits an afghan
or sews a gown.
So whenever I see her take it down

I think of the things
my dolls could wear
of whatever my Grandmother has to spare.

## The Hill

My great-grandparents
lie
on a hill
where the wind blows soft
and it's
very
still;
and we read their names
on the marble squares,
and my grandmother
moves her lips
in prayers.
There is a bench
made of grainy stone
where my grandmother goes
to sit
alone,
while my mother
pulls the grass that grows
over the names
and lays a rose
on
every
grave
where it tells the years;
and my
mother and grandmother
hug,
with tears.

## Coming From Kansas

Whenever they come from Kansas
they stay for nearly a week
and they live with Grandma in Council Bluffs
because her house has room enough,
and we go over the day they arrive.
Everyone shouts when they pull in the drive.
We kiss and hug and I get to play
with my cousin Joan most every day

    *and the grown-ups cry when they leave.*

Whenever they say they're coming,
we make a lot of plans.
Joan and I like to put on a play
and we start to write it the very first day.
There're costumes and sets and curtains to do;
we write a part for the neighbor boy, too,
Denny, who comes in the very first scene
to introduce Joan, who's always the queen

    *and I have to be the king.*

And when it's hot in the afternoons
we get a big glass of Kool-Aid
and play cribbage or jacks on the vestibule floor
and Denny, the boy who lives next door,
comes over and dares us to go up the hill
where the cemetery, dark and still,
lies spooky with ghosts. We go before night,
but Denny and Joan always get in a fight

    *and I have to take Joan's side.*

Whenever they come in summer,

Joan tells me about her friends.
She says that Kansas is better, too,
there's always more fun and things to do.
But when we visited there last year
I saw her friends, and they all were queer,
And I told her so, and her face got tight
And then we had a terrible fight

*and we pulled each other's hair.*

When we go to Grandma's in autumn,
Joan isn't there any more,
And Denny comes over. There's so much to do
like racing down North Second Avenue
or daring each other to slide down the eaves
or sloshing the puddles and jumping in leaves
and if we decide to write out a scene
Denny will always let me be queen

*and I don't have to bother with Joan!*

## Fletcher Avenue

In my
grandmother's house
sun comes through leaded panes
on the front stair landing, creeping
softly

over
the red carpet,
flashing yellow circles
and white dots, with ribbons of blue
dancing

on the
bannisters and
balconies, coming to
rest on warm wood walls in the dark
hallways.

## Lemonade Stand

Every summer
under the shade
we fix up a stand
to sell lemonade.

A stack of cups,
a pitcher of ice,
a shirtboard sign
to tell the price.

A dime for the big,
A nickel for small.
The nickel cup's short.
The dime cup's tall.

Plenty of sugar
to make it sweet,
and sometimes cookies
for us to eat.

But when the sun
moves into the shade
it gets too hot
to sell lemonade.

Nobody stops
so we put things away
and drink what's left
and start to play.

*Lena*

Lena
is leaving
to marry a man
somewhere off
in Oregon;
a man who writes to her
every day
and asked her to come to the West
to stay.

Lena
says
it may take some time,
but when she's married
it will be fine.
She's taking
her comforter filled with down
to a house
she can always call
her own.

Lena
says
we can visit her there.
And she's bought
a brand-new coat
to wear,
and as soon as she gets off the train
she'll call,
and she says
not to worry ourselves
at all.

All of us
cried
when she came down the stairs
from the upstairs room
where she's lived for years,
and even Grandfather
said goodbye
with a gruffy voice
and wet
in his eye.

Grandmother
says
it won't be the same
when Lena takes
that foreign man's name,
and why couldn't Lena
marry a man
a little bit closer
than Oregon?

## Up North Second

The statue
of Our Lady
stands
praying
there
with folded hands.

Silently,
eyes closed,
she waits,
shut behind
tall
iron gates.

White and cool,
she prays for hours,
lost
among the
graveyard
flowers.

## Secret Passageway

Near the lilac bush
there's a passageway
where my friend Jan
can come over and play.

We've a secret word
that we whisper there,
and it lets us know
when the coast is clear,

and Jan waits there
on the other side
and we part the leaves
so the path is wide

and she hurries through
where the branches split,
and the lilacs tremble
a little bit.

## Big House

Someday when we're older,
Someday when we're grown,
Dick Minard and I plan to marry.
We'll want a big house
with a hill for a lawn
like Aunt Blanche and Uncle Harry.
We'll have three bay windows,
a storm porch in winter,
a sunroom with chairs of bamboo,
a small secret closet like Harriet has
and a cubbyhole desk painted blue.

We'll have a big planter
with white cupids dancing,
a huge painting hung on the wall,
and a piano to play
with a fringed scarf draped over,
a grandfather clock in the hall.
And both of my cousins,
Harriet, Frances,
will want to come visit our home,
and see our bay windows
and piano and sunporch
and say it looks just like their own.

## Aunt Flora (*Envoi*)

In her
new apartment,
Aunt Flora keeps the past:
the singing piano and the
love seat

from the
dim green parlor,
the hard brown rocker with
lion faces for arms, old books
read in

summer,
and the china
with faded flowers, and
Aunt Flora, Aunt Flora, waiting
for me.